VIDEOS

KAY ROWLEY

ROCK WORLD

Crestwood House
New York

ROCK WORLD

ROCK CONCERTS
ROCK MUSIC
ROCK STARS
ROCK VIDEOS

EDITOR: James Kerr
SERIES DESIGNER: Helen White
COVER: Madonna is a rock star who is well known for her videos.

First published in Great Britain in 1991 by
Wayland (Publishers) Ltd
61 Western Road, Hove
East Sussex BN3 1JD

First published in the United States in 1992 by
Crestwood House
Macmillan Publishing Company
866 Third Avenue
New York, NY 10022

Macmillan Publishing Company is part of the Maxwell
Macmillan Communication Group of Companies

First Edition
Printed in Italy by G. Canale & C.S.p.A., Turin
10 9 8 7 6 5 4 3 2 1

Rowley, Kay.
   Rock Videos / by Kay Rowley. — 1st ed.
      p.   cm. — (Rock world)
   Includes bibliographical references and index.
   Summary: Describes the costly and creative process of making videos to promote
rock music and performers.
   ISBN 0-89686-712-9
   1. Music videos—Production and direction— Juvenile literature.
 [1. Music videos—Production and direction.   2. Rock music.]
 I. Title.   II. Series.
PN1992.8.M87R68   1992
791.45'023—dc20   91-15073
                                                                       CIP
                                                                        AC

CONTENTS

INTRO

IN MANY WAYS the video revolution of the 1980s did for rock stars what the introduction of sound to movies in the 1920s did for movie stars. It added a new dimension to the artists' performances.

However, some of the silent movie stars could not make the transition to "talkies." Some, for example, had strong foreign accents. Similarly, the demands of making a convincing and entertaining video have helped to sort out the real rock stars from the "also-rans."

In some instances, of course, the star of the video has been the director rather than the artist. However, if you look back at the outstanding videos of the last ten years, you will see most have been made by performers who understand what a powerful promotional tool video is. These artists have jumped at the chance to star in their own three-minute movies.

Record companies have long been aware that to make an artist into a star, the performer has to be seen as well as heard. The usual route was to star a popular singer in a full-length musical feature film, often with little or no story line. This was a way to promote his or her latest release.

By the beginning of the 1950s in the United States, there were already music shows on TV hosted by popular bandleaders. Rock and roll, in the person of Elvis Presley, exploded on the scene a few years later. When rumors of Elvis's ecstatic fan following reached the ears of TV executives, he was invited to perform his latest hit, "Hound Dog," on TV. He caused a sensation.

Film companies rushed to cash in on the latest trend. By mid-1957 there were 25 full-length movies starring rock and roll artists such as Little Richard and Bill Haley. In Great Britain in 1958, the TV show *Oh Boy!* was launched, making a star of Cliff Richard.

By 1960 Hollywood had given up on rock movies, leaving only Elvis and Cliff to continue making their musicals. However, the Beatles' enormous success on the *Ed Sullivan Show* once more revived interest in presenting rock music on TV.

The development of lip-synching in the early 1960s gave stars like the Rolling Stones much more freedom to move around the set. In the past they had been rooted behind microphones. In some cases, however, stars were not available to appear live on TV. Instead, short performance films were shot and inserted into shows.

Jason Donovan
on the set of the
Rhythm of the
Rain *video.*

FIRST VIDEOS

BY THE MID-1960s groups like the Beatles and the Rolling Stones had become international stars, undertaking worldwide tours. These stars made promotional films (promos), which could be shown on TV while the bands were touring.

Some promos were put together in a hurry, with little or no plot or any real direction. Many were basic performance films shot in a studio against a simple backdrop. The group mimed to the record. However, there were a few groups who wanted to get away from this restricted setup. By 1966 both the Kinks and the Who had made promos in which they neither played nor lip-synched. For *Dead-End Street*, the Kinks appeared as undertakers. For *Happy Jack*, the Who ran around dressed as burglars trying to crack a safe.

As befitted their rebellious image, the Rolling Stones made what were considered very daring promos at the time. In 1966 they appeared dressed as women in the promo *Have You Seen Your Mother, Baby, Standing in the Shadows*. The Beatles, on the other hand, favored a more gentle, often humorous approach to their

Early promos featured groups like the Beatles miming to records.

promos. By 1967 they were no longer touring. To satisfy their American fans, they had a special film shot for their double-sided hit "Strawberry Fields Forever" / "Penny Lane."

The Monkees' TV series, which started in 1966, drew heavily from the Beatles. It also relied on a lot of montage photography with very little plot. Nevertheless, the band's crazy adventures proved a huge success all over the world. It helped them achieve ten gold records in just under two years.

In the mid-1970s, avant-garde groups in America, like the Residents and Devo, started making their own promos. Many of these early videos looked like home movies. However, things were about to change.

Toward the end of 1975, EMI released a six-minute-long semi-operatic single entitled "Bohemian Rhapsody." It was by one of the company's most up-and-coming bands, Queen. Selecting such a long cut as a single was quite a gamble. To help with its promotion, the record company commissioned director Bruce Gowers to make a video to accompany the single. The film

used trailing images of the band's disembodied heads, together with live-performance footage. It reputedly cost $6,000 to make. It was quickly hailed by the press as a masterpiece. The film had a lasting impression on viewers who saw it on television. It also helped keep the record at number one on the British charts for nine weeks.

On the strength of this success, Gowers joined forces with another filmmaker, Jon Roseman. They set about trying to convince record companies that videos were the shape of things to come. During the following three years, Roseman's company successfully cornered the video market both in Great Britain and in America. It

Some of today's groups like the House of Love have made videos similar to the promos of the 1960s.

made videos for stars such as David Essex, Genesis, Rod Stewart and Elton John.

By mid-1979, Roseman's company had shot over 180 promos and had taken on two new directors: Russell Mulcahy and David Mallet. These directors had directed videos for many of the bands who were at the forefront of the new wave/punk movement of the late 1970s, such as the Sex Pistols, the Stranglers and the Boomtown Rats. In some of these videos, Mulcahy in particular pioneered many of the techniques and effects that have since become commonplace. These include split screen and triple screen edits, objects smashing in slow motion, and tight close-ups.

In 1979 Casey Casem's *American Top Ten* became the first network TV show to play videos regularly in the United States, followed by NBC's *Friday Nite Videos*. Two years later MTV was launched, and by 1985 it boasted over 18 million viewers nationwide.

The effect of MTV on record sales was amazing. By 1983 record sales were soaring as TV stations in America started showing music videos. In Great Britain, however, there were far fewer video outlets. Because companies like the BBC were reluctant to feature bands on TV, videos were slow to take off. MTV Europe was launched in 1987 but is still limited to Sky Channel subscribers, who number only a few million. It is a far cry from the current American MTV audience of 48 million.

Many punk videos were performance films, though they had a more aggressive feel than the promos of the 1960s.

M.C. Hammer receives an MTV award.

MAKING VIDEOS

THE EARLIEST PROMOS were made very much on a shoestring budget of around $400 to $1,000, either in a studio or on location, with one or two technicians and a 16 mm camera. They were usually pretty disorganized affairs, since no one really knew what they were doing. A lot of time was wasted trying to get things right.

The filmmakers were often just friends of the group. They were usually connected in some way with the film or television industry and made the videos in their spare time. As they gained experience and saw that more could be done with this particular format, they left their jobs and formed video companies.

By the end of the 1970s, record companies were regularly using videos to help promote their record releases. They realized that videos could be used both to launch a new act and to help an established one maintain or change its image. In order to do this, the films had to have a definite story line. This was drawn up on storyboards, which could be acted out by the band.

One of the first bands of the 1980s to use comedy successfully was Madness, a north London group well known for their crazy on-stage antics. Between 1979 and 1985 the band chalked up 21 hit singles in Great Britain, very much with the help of their amusing and inventive videos. For their *Shut Up* video in 1981, they drew their inspiration from the silent films of the 1920s featuring the Keystone Kops. The lead singer, Suggs, played a masked villain pursued by the rest of the band, who were dressed as policemen. In *Baggy Trousers*, saxophonist Lee Thompson was suspended by invisible wires from a crane, so that he appeared to be playing in midair.

Storyboarding is one of the most important steps in creating an interesting and effective video, and is usually the task of the director. Once the record company has decided upon the release date of the single in question, a tape of the record is then sent to various video production companies. The producers will then meet with the record company and the band. They will play them films made by a number of video directors, so that the band can decide who will be best for the job.

The choice of director depends on various factors: who is available at the time, what the record company has in mind and how much money it wants to spend. Next, the chosen director will meet with the record company and the band to discuss what sort of image or message the video should convey. Then he or she will go away to prepare what is called a "treatment." Usually this is one or two pages of ideas that outline the story, or scenario. The director

ABOVE: Image and design are two key ingredients in video production.

LEFT: Queen dressed up in drag for their I Want to Break Free *video.*

OPPOSITE: Madness made some of the most original videos of the 1980s.

David Bowie works closely with the directors of his videos to make sure that they are original and unusual.

left to chance. The more complex the action, the more essential it is for everything to run smoothly.

Sometimes the band will contribute their own ideas toward the video, but mostly artistic control is in the hands of the director. In a few cases, the artist has a much greater say. For instance, David Bowie often chooses who will direct his videos, and he often works as co-scriptwriter. In even rarer instances the artist takes complete control. David Lee Roth not only writes his own storyboards but also directs, produces and pays for the videos himself.

While the video is being shot, the director will frequently look through the camera lens. At the same time, he or she consults the storyboard to make sure there is continuity. This is especially important in location shooting, where the weather can change suddenly. It would look odd if in one scene the action took place in bright sunshine, while in the next it was suddenly overcast or raining!

When the shooting is completed, the film is then developed and transferred onto videotape. Then it can be edited together with the sound, ready for release.

looks for ideas that will suit both the band and the song.

The treatment is submitted to the record company for approval, and if everyone is in agreement, the director will set about scripting the film in detail. By drawing up the story frame-by-frame, the director is able to transfer onto paper the images and scenes he or she has in mind. This ensures that nothing is

ABOVE: *David Lee Roth's* California Girls *video – featuring lots of girls in bikinis – is typical of those by heavy metal artists. Many people criticize such videos for their negative protrayal of women.*

LEFT: *Jason Donovan getting in on the act.*

LIVE VIDEO

LIVE VIDEOS used to be seen as a way of capturing bands on film without a record company having to spend huge amounts of money. A band on tour or in rehearsal would simply be filmed playing their latest single, and that was that.

As videos became more sophisticated, many groups preferred to make "concept" videos. In these they acted rather than played, projecting themselves as stylists rather than musicians. However, there remained plenty of other artists whose greatest asset was the power of their live shows. Some of the fans would not readily accept their fooling around with "artistic" videos.

One case in point was Bruce Springsteen. He admitted that he felt uncomfortable and self-conscious in a non-performance video like *Tunnel of Love*, whereas he felt much more at home performing "Dancing in the Dark" on stage.

Live action is also a crucial ingredient in the appeal of heavy metal bands. It's rare to see them on video not playing at top volume before an adoring audience. Occasionally, heavy metal acts will send themselves up on video, for example, Aerosmith on Run DMC's

Bon Jovi have used the live performance video to good effect.

Walk This Way or Van Halen in the video for "Jump." But usually the furthest they stray from the live video is a mimed performance on a large studio stage set in which they still have enough room to strut and pose.

Of course, many "live" videos aren't live at all but are set up before a specially selected audience who look as if they are at a real concert. To ensure a continuously enthusiastic reaction during the eight hours it took to shoot the video for "I'm Your Man," Wham! invited their fan club to fill London's Marquee Club. Similarly, for *Radio Gaga*, hundreds of Queen fans were drilled to wave their hands in unison during the group's "performance" on a giant studio set.

One rather sneaky trick often used by video directors for newer heavy metal bands is to shoot them at all-day open air festivals. With

Some heavy metal videos incorporate images from horror movies.

Madonna's Ciao Italia *video.*

What a record company spends on making a video depends very much on what it expects to make in profit from the sales of both the record and the video itself. Shooting concert or tour performances, therefore, offers them a cost-effective way of prolonging the public's interest in a record after the initial buzz has died down. Good examples of this are two of the top-selling videos from 1988, Madonna's *Ciao Italia – Live from Italy* and Bros' *The Live Big Push Tour.*

The average cost of making a video in 1990 was about $75,000. Of this, 15 to 20 percent goes to the production company, 10 percent to the director, 5 percent to the producer and the rest is spent on making and editing the video.

Videos can be made for as little as $30,000 but these are usually pretty basic. Perhaps they will use local street scenes for outside locations or straightforward camera work in a studio. For $60,000 the video can include a few props and extras, alternating with studio or live performance. However, in order to go on location to another country or to make an entirely conceptual video with all the trimmings, the budget needs to be

careful editing, it often looks as though the huge audience is there just for them. The giveaway is if they are performing in daylight. If they were truly the main attraction, instead of just a warm-up act, they would not be on until at least dusk, if not later!

at least $100,000. After this, the sky is the limit.

For Elton John's 1983 video *I'm Still Standing*, director Russell Mulcahy's budget was unspecified, which was probably just as well. On the very first afternoon of shooting in the South of France, dozens of costumes for the huge cast of dancers had to be replaced at short notice and shipped over from England. By the time the video was ready for transmission, the whole production had cost $300,000. At today's rates this would be something in the region of $500,000 just for three minutes of film!

ABOVE: The Stone Roses are one of a number of new bands who keep their videos fairly simple to suit their stripped-down image.

LEFT: Elton John has made various types of videos. His I'm Still Standing *video featured elaborate costumes and choreography.*

ANIMATION

THE ART OF animation was revived in the 1980s. In Great Britain, companies like Cosgrove Hall have enjoyed great success with TV series such as *The Wind in the Willows, Count Duckula* and *Dangermouse*. In the United States, film producer Steven Spielberg has made one full-length animated feature movie, *An American Tail*, and a mixed live and cartoon movie, *Who Framed Roger Rabbit?* This won an Oscar for its animation.

With the success of the movie *Teenage Mutant Ninja Turtles*, the popularity of movies featuring animation and actors in costume seems set to continue in the 1990s. Used in rock videos, animation integrated with live action gives a director another dimension in which to work. Animation makes it possible to conjure up surreal images or gravity-defying action. In A-Ha's video *Take on Me*, for example, transforming lead singer Morten into a graphic image

allowed him to walk through a mirror straight into a cartoon story.

One of the most ambitious music videos to use animation in recent years was Peter Gabriel's award-winning *Sledgehammer*. During the two-week shoot, Gabriel was required to sit for two days before a camera, making various facial contortions in the appropriate makeup for a process called pixilation. This is speeded up action by live actors. This footage was then matched to the animated model sequences. For example, in one scene it appears that Gabriel's eyes are following a model steam train that is running around his head. In another scene, an ice model of Gabriel's head is cleverly substituted so that the sledgehammer can smash what looks like his real head.

Using animation is a fairly expensive business because it is labor intensive and the editing needs to be expertly handled. For *Sledgehammer*, the animation company's fee was in the area of $40,000. This just about covered the cost of employing two model makers, three sculptors, eight animators, six scenic artists, a costume designer and makeup artist, six camera operators and a

lighting specialist.

Mixing animation and live action so that it looks convincing, artistically as well as technically, depends a lot on how much the artist is prepared to throw him or herself into the fantasy scenes. Singers who have previous acting or dancing experience or who are good stage performers naturally have a head start. Three good examples are Cyndi Lauper (*She-Bop*), Madonna (*Who's That Girl*) and Paula Abdul.

In her video for "Opposites Attract," Abdul dances with an animated life-size cat. In the movie *Anchors Aweigh*, dancer Gene Kelly partnered Jerry Mouse (of *Tom and Jerry* fame) in a dance

OPPOSITE AND ABOVE: The popularity of animation in the late 1980s and early 1990s – as seen in the success of Who Framed Roger Rabbit? *– is reflected in rock videos.*

routine. It required both characters to use exactly the same steps. To achieve this, Kelly's live action was first filmed, then rotoscoped – that is, traced onto animation paper – so that Jerry could be drawn doing exactly the same movements. Much of this sort of thing can now be done by computer. In 1944, when the movie was made, it was all done by hand.

Animation in videos is artistically exciting. It can also be used to solve problems. When exposure on a TV commercial for hot chocolate turned Nina Simone's "My Baby Just Cares for Me" into an unexpected hit in Great Britain, the artist was not at that time signed to a record deal. Since it is the record companies that, in the majority of cases, foot the bill for videos, a solution was needed that didn't require the artist's presence. The answer was to make an animated story instead. It was made by Aardman Animations, which produced the *Sledgehammer* video.

Jackie Wilson's 1957 hit "Reet Petite" was re-released in Great Britain in 1987 and became a surprise number one hit. Since the singer had died, an alternative idea for a video had to be found. Animation came to the rescue, and the video – with its models of singing lips on legs and saxophones that come to life – became as big a hit as the record.

A ROCK SINGER who can move well is always more interesting to watch than one who just stands still. This can be tough on stars who are not natural dancers. They often go through agony trying to learn dance steps for TV specials or live shows.

Since the advent of video, standing still is no longer an option. Viewers have had their expectations raised over the last decade. They now require someone to do more than shuffle about in an uncoordinated way.

Many performers incorporate well-choreographed dance routines in their live acts. These stars – such as Michael Jackson, Madonna or Prince – have a distinct advantage, and video gives them the freedom to show off their skills.

Of course, some stars who make dance records get over the problem by having professional dancers help them out. For Lionel Richie's 1986 *Dancing on the Ceiling* video, director Stanley Donen inserted a trick sequence from a

American rappers Full Force on location in New York City.

21

The dance moves in M.C. Hammer's videos are as important as the music.

choreographer on TV shows in the 1960s, Basil went on to choreograph tours for David Bowie and Bette Midler. For *Mickey*, she used her own experience as a college cheerleader. Some split screen and miniaturization effects allow her to dance with herself. Her success foreshadowed that of another former cheerleader who has used her dancing experience to good effect – Paula Abdul. She started out as a cheerleader for the L.A. Lakers.

Two of the most ground-breaking videos featuring dance sequences were Michael Jackson's *Beat It* and *Thriller*. Jackson had been spinning and dipping on stage like a junior James Brown since his childhood days with the Jackson 5. It seemed a natural progression to incorporate his best moves into his videos.

For megastar Jackson, money is no object. To direct the spoof horror mini-movie for *Thriller*, film director John Landis, who had made the movie *An American Werewolf in London*, was brought in. The zombie dance routine devised by Michael Peters (who also choreographed *Beat It*) set new standards by which other dance-oriented videos would be measured.

1951 movie, *Royal Wedding*. In this movie Fred Astaire dances across the ceiling and down the walls. In Whitney Houston's video *I Want to Dance with Somebody*, she merely stands by while a succession of male dancers expend all their energy.

One of the first dance-oriented videos to break new ground was Toni Basil's *Mickey*, made back in 1980. From her start as a

Jackson, however, has not been without competition. Paula Abdul has become very influential. She has provided exciting routines for Janet Jackson's "Rhythm Nation" and "Miss You Much" hits as well as her own hits "Straight Up" and "Opposites Attract."

Madonna spent two years with Alvin Ailey's dance company before turning to singing. She is another artist who makes good use of her early training. One of her most ambitious videos was for "Material Girl." In this she faithfully re-created Marilyn Monroe's "Diamonds Are a Girl's Best Friend" routine from the movie *Gentlemen Prefer Blondes*.

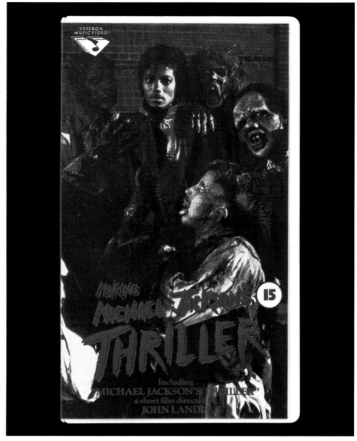

For her 1990 hit "Vogue," Madonna brought dance right up to date by using the latest New York dance fashion, "voguing."

In a completely different but equally exciting style are teenage megastars New Kids on the Block. They incorporate street-sharp dance and rap routines into their videos. This has helped them sell 2 million copies of their *Hanging Tough Live* video, released at the end of 1989.

ABOVE: The Thriller *video was so popular that* Making Michael Jackson's "Thriller" *was released as a home video.*

LEFT: Janet Jackson's Rhythm Nation *video was choreographed by Paula Abdul.*

23

RIGHT: Neneh Cherry incorporates dance into many of her videos.

OPPOSITE: Simon Le Bon in Duran Duran's Rio video.

SOMETIMES WHEN you watch a video, it seems as though the action on screen has a life of its own and does not obviously relate to the song's lyrics. This is what is called a concept video. There can be all sorts of reasons for this. Sometimes the lyrics themselves are abstract rather than narrative. In this case, the director must dream up a fantasy scenario that will complement the song by creating the right mood.

Prime examples of this are the videos made for Duran Duran by director Russell Mulcahy. For *Hungry Like the Wolf, Save a Prayer* and *Rio*, Mulcahy chose to shoot on location in Sri Lanka and Antigua. This meant the action took place in another, more exotic place, where anything could happen. In *Hungry Like the Wolf*, singer Simon Le Bon is seen pursuing a beautiful woman through jungles and local markets as though he is on the trail of a wild animal. In the last sequence, she turns on him. It is left to the viewer's own imagination to decide whether the hunter has been captured by the hunted instead of the other way around.

This freedom to explore imagery has also been used to good effect by artists like David Bowie. He has used his own interest in the theater and mime to add drama to his videos. He usually closely collaborates on the script with the director. Sometimes the action is hard to follow, but the visuals themselves are always striking.

One of his most ambitious videos was *Ashes to Ashes*. It was shot in Australia. Bowie appears first as a white-faced clown and then as an older version of his Major Tom character from an earlier hit, *Space Oddity*. Director David Mallet used weird camera angles, solarization and saturated color to create a surreal, other-worldly effect. This was heightened by Bowie holding a postcard-size video screen displaying the first shot of the next scene.

CONCEPT VIDEO

ABOVE: *Many of the Cure's videos are surreal.*

OPPOSITE BELOW: *Kylie Minogue's* I Should Be So Lucky *video made use of graphics.*

cameo appearances by celebrities like Dan Aykroyd, Whoopi Goldberg, Steven Spielberg, Rosanna Arquette and John Travolta. As the song ends, Jackson – who has been secretly filming the whole thing from an elevated crane – swoops down, much to everyone's surprise, and calls it a wrap.

These days concept videos are usually some of the most expensive to make. This is because so much is done at post-production stage. If the video is a complex one, the director may sit down and talk with the film editors before the shoot. They discuss how certain effects can be achieved on camera. This will save the cost of adding the effects artificially. Sometimes, however, it is the skill and imagination of the off- and on-line editors that can turn a good video into an inspired one.

Off-line editing is the process of combining the film and the soundtrack, editing out the mistakes and coming up with what is called a rough cut. At this stage, the unfinished video can be shown to the record company for approval before more work is done.

The video itself is shot on film. Attached to the film is a time code

Not all concept videos are so artistic – some are just good fun. An excellent example is Michael Jackson's *Liberian Girl*. As the song starts up, we are on a movie set surrounded by well-known personalities waiting for Jackson to appear so that shooting of the video can begin. Unseen, the camera moves around, picking up snatches of conversation and

numbering each frame of each reel. The separate soundtrack is coded in exactly the same way, so that the editor can make sure the action is synchronized with the music. Sorting through hours of footage can take up to a week, depending on the complexity of the video. To keep costs down, this stage of the editing is usually carried out on cheaper film.

Once the editing is complete, and the director and producer are happy with the result, the video is sent to an on-line editing room, where the rough cut edits are applied to a better tape called broadcast quality tape. This can then be edited further and any special effects can be added.

The range of special effects is enormous and is limited only by the time and money that can be spent.

ABOVE: It is important to get things like lighting and camera angles right.

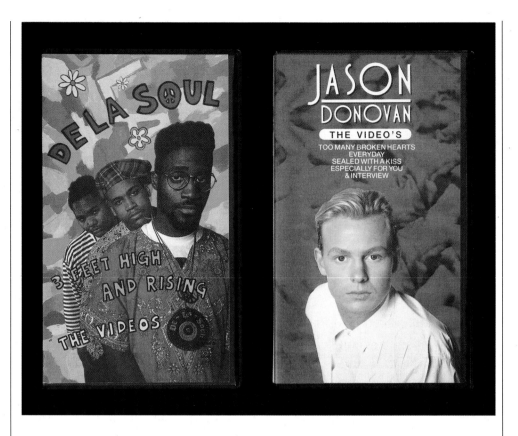

For example, a singer can be filmed against a particular colored background, say, blue. A computer can be programmed to erase the color blue whenever it appears. This leaves the performer as a stencil, seemingly suspended in midair, and then any sort of background can be added. This could be an animated sequence. Or it might be a painted backdrop that is tweaked electronically to move around, like the brightly colored patterns on the Technotronic video for "Pump Up the Jam."

If the images to be applied are photographic or graphic, they are usually refined by the use of a paint box. This is a computer that allows the artist to transform electronically, the size, color and style of a drawing or photograph. Paint boxes can also be used to create simple animation.

Another of the computerized processes available to the on-line editor is multilayering. This is where lots of images can be superimposed, so that they appear to walk around the singer or float across the screen. Finding the right  to put the images up a post-production studio can run into millions of dollars.

Since its introduction some three or four years ago, digital recording has done for videos what the CD did for audio reproduction a few years before. Endless copies can be made without any loss of quality, so that the video you buy is as good as the original mastertape. Unfortunately, the current home television receiver is not able to transmit these videos in their full glory. It will be some time before newly developed models that are able to do this will be available to the consumer.

GLOSSARY

Abstract   Dealing with ideas and not events.

Audio   Pertaining to the broadcast of sound.

Avant-garde   Ahead of its time.

Budget   The amount of money put aside to make the video.

Cameo appearance   A small but important part in a film.

Choreography   The design or arrangement of dance steps.

Collaborate   To work closely with someone else.

Cost-effective   Getting one's money's worth.

Edit   To remove by cutting.

Graphic   Image drawn with a pencil or pen, or on screen.

Lip-synching   Abbreviation of lip synchronize, i.e., moving the lips in time to the words of the song.

Mastertape   The finished tape of the video, containing both the sound and the pictures, on which no mistakes remain.

Mime   To act with gestures using no speech.

Montage   A composition or picture consisting of various images placed next to or partially on top of one another.

Narrative   Telling a story or recounting events.

On location   A place outside the studio where a movie or video is shot.

Post-production   The editing that takes place after the video has been filmed.

Punk   Fashion and music of the late 1970s characterized by ripped clothing and aggression.

Rough cut   The unfinished, or test, version of the video.

Saturate   To intensify artificially.

Scenario   An outline, or sketch, of the story.

Shoot   The actual filming of a video.

Solarization   The burning effect on the negative film by overexposure to the sun.

Soundtrack   The narrow strip at one side of a film that carries the sound recording.

Split screen edit   Where the screen is divided into several parts to show different things going on at the same time.

Stencil   An outline or shape.

Storyboard   A drawn plan of each scene of the video.

Superimpose   To lay one image or object over another.

Surreal   Dreamlike, fantastical.

Transmission   Sending a picture or message by light or sound waves.

Wrap   A successfully filmed sequence.

READING LIST

Blocher, Arlo. *Rock*. New Jersey: Troll, 1976.

Busnar, Gene. *It's Rock 'n' Roll*. New York: Messner, 1979.

Bygrave, Mike. *Rock*. London: Hamilton, 1977.

David, Andrew. *Rock Stars: People at the Top of the Charts*. New York: Exeter Books, 1979.

Fornatale, Peter. *The Story of Rock 'n' Roll*. New York: William Morrow, 1987.

Lane, Peter. *What Rock Is All About*. New York: Messner, 1979.

Meigs, James B. and Jennifer Stern. *Make Your Own Music Video*. New York: Franklin Watts, 1986.

MTV Presents 2nd Annual MTV Video Music Awards. New Jersey: Warner Bros. Publications, 1985.

Nite, Norm N. *Rock On: The Illustrated Encyclopedia of Rock 'n' Roll: The Video Revolution, 1978-Present*. New York: Harper & Row, 1985.

Paige, David. *A Day in the Life of a Rock Musician*. New Jersey: Troll, 1980.

Van der Horst, Brian. *Rock Music*. New York: Franklin Watts, 1973.

White, Timothy. *Rock Stars*. New York: Stewart, Tabori & Chang, 1984.

PICTURE ACKNOWLEDGMENTS

All Action Pictures (L. Cotteral) 9, (Robin Kennedy) 24, (Robin Kennedy) 27 (top); Aquarius Picture Library 10, 12, 14, 25, 27 (bottom); London Features International Ltd. 5, 11 (bottom), (A. Vereecke) 13 (top), 13 (bottom), (Olleren Shaw) 17 (bottom), 21, (Kevin Mazur) 22, 26; National Film Archive 19; Redferns (Suzi Gibbons) 7, (Mike Prior) 11 (top), (Fin Costello) 15; Rex Features Limited (Stephen Harvey) 20; Paul Seheult 16, 23 (top), 28, 29; Topham 6, 8, 17 (top); Wayland Picture Library 18.

READING LIST

INDEX